Kayla and Kugel

By Ann D. Koffsky

This **PJ BOOK** belongs to

_____

_____

PJ Library®

JEWISH BEDTIME STORIES and SONGS

For my husband, Mark,
who has made everything
I do possible.

You are a true *gibor chayil*.
Thank you.

—ADK

Apples & Honey Press
An imprint of Behrman House and Gefen Publishing House
Behrman House, 11 Edison Place, Springfield, New Jersey 07081
Gefen Publishing House Ltd., 6 Hatzvi Street, Jerusalem 94386, Israel
www.applesandhoneypress.com

Copyright © 2015 by Ann D. Koffsky

ISBN 978-1-68115-502-9

All rights reserved. No part of this publication may be translated,
reproduced, stored in a retrieval system or transmitted, in any form or
by any means, electronic, mechanical, photocopying, recording or otherwise,
without express written permission from the publishers.

Library of Congress Cataloging-in-Publication Data
Koffsky, Ann D., author, illustrator.
Kayla and Kugel / by Ann Koffsky.
pages cm
Summary: Kayla and her mischievous dog Kugel set the table for Shabbat
but something is missing—family. Includes note to parents about Shabbat
and the Jewish values of Hiddur Mitzvah and Sh'lom Bayit.
ISBN 978-1-68115-502-9
[1. Table setting and decoration—Fiction. 2. Dogs—Fiction. 3. Sabbath—Fiction.
4. Judaism—Customs and practices—Fiction. 5. Commandments (Judaism)—Fiction.] I. Title.
PZ7.K81935Kay 2015
[E]—dc23
2014040108

Design by Elynn Cohen
Edited by Dena Neusner
Printed in China
1 3 5 7 9 8 6 4 2

101511.7K1/B0615/A2

I'm Kayla and this is my dog, Kugel.
Today we are going to set the
table for Shabbat.

Hi!

Careful, Kugel! Don't get paw prints on the bright white tablecloth.

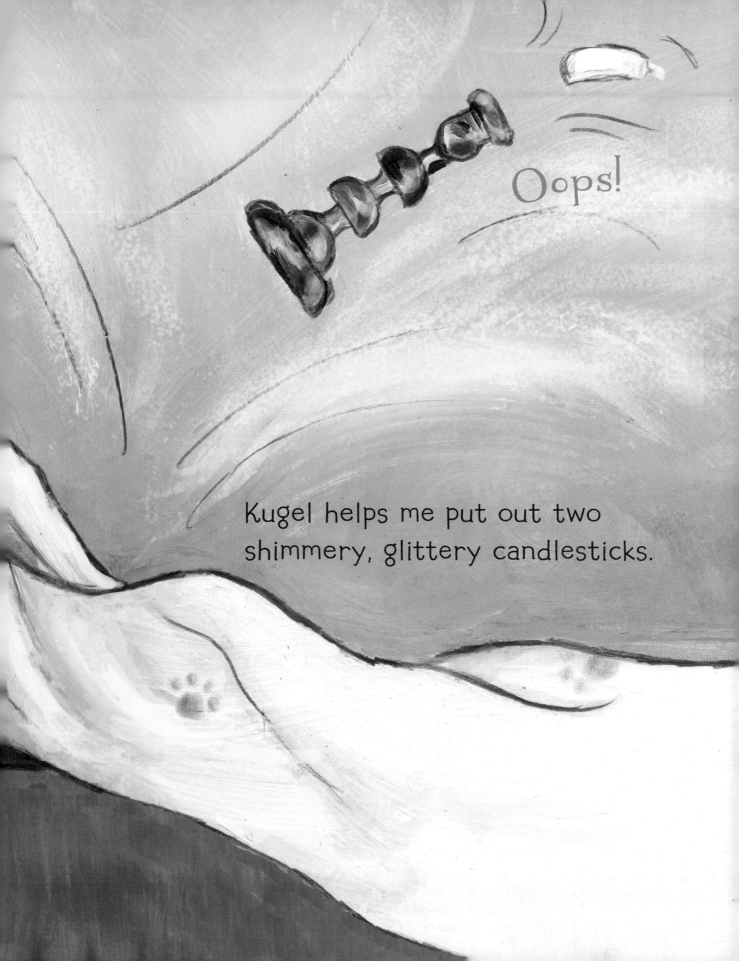

Oops!

Kugel helps me put out two shimmery, glittery candlesticks.

And two toasty, twisted challahs. Hey, the Kiddush cup is missing! Where did it go?

Kugel! Give the Kiddush cup back!

Careful,
Kugel!

These are the fancy shmancy plates.

Kugel brings the shaky, tasty salt.

I pour the purple, sweet grape juice.

These flowers smell delicious.
Kugel, don't eat that!

We're all ready for Shabbat!
I couldn't have done it
without you, Kugel.

What's wrong, Kugel?
What are we missing?

Shabbat is best when we share it with family.

NOW we're all ready.

Shabbat shalom!

Dear Friends,

Kugel has got it right—No Shabbat is complete without family. The Jewish value of *sh'lom bayit* means creating peace in the home. Shabbat creates a weekly sanctuary in time, a day of rest that is the ideal time to connect with family and build a loving and peaceful home.

Kayla has got it right, too—The key to making a beautiful Shabbat is using special things set aside and used just for Shabbat. They don't need to be fancy shmancy, and might include a homemade challah cover, or a Kiddush cup decorated with glue, rhinestones, and love. This idea is known in Hebrew as *hiddur mitzvah*, using beauty to enhance a religious practice.

After reading *Kayla and Kugel*, talk with your child about these ideas:

How can you make Shabbat fancy, shmancy, and beautiful? What is your favorite thing to do with family? Why?

Download a free Kayla and Kugel activity page from www.annkoffsky.com and decorate your home and table for Shabbat.

Shabbat shalom,

Ann